THE BEAST
BENEATH THE STAIRS

LD

BY MICHAEL DAHL
ILLUSTRATED BY PATRICIA MOFFETT

Librarian Reviewer
Laurie K. Holland
Media Specialist (National Board Certified), Edina, MN
MA in Elementary Education, Minnesota State University, Mankato

Reading Consultant
Elizabeth Stedem
Educator/Consultant, Colorado Springs, CO
MA in Elementary Education, University of Denver, CO

STONE ARCH BOOKS
Minneapolis San Diego

Zone Books are published by Stone Arch Books,
151 Good Counsel Drive, P.O. Box 669,
Mankato, Minnesota 56002.
www.stonearchbooks.com

Copyright © 2007 by Stone Arch Books

Library of Congress Cataloging-in-Publication Data
Dahl, Michael.
  The Beast Beneath the Stairs / by Michael Dahl; illustrated
by Patricia Moffett.
  p. cm. — (Zone Books - Library of Doom)
  Summary: When the Librarian returns to his castle after
lengthy travels, he finds that someone has stolen his collection
of deadly books, and until he can get past a beast the thief left
behind and track them down, the world is in great jeopardy.
  ISBN-13: 978-1-59889-323-6 (library binding)
  ISBN-10: 1-59889-323-8 (library binding)
  ISBN-13: 978-1-59889-418-9 (paperback)
  ISBN-10: 1-59889-418-8 (paperback)
  [1. Books and reading—Fiction. 2. Librarians—Fiction.
3. Monsters—Fiction. 4. Fantasy.] I. Moffett, Patricia, ill.
II. Title.
PZ7.D15134Bea 2007
[Fic]—dc22   2006027529

Art Director: Heather Kindseth
Cover Graphic Designer: Brann Garvey
Interior Graphic Designer: Kay Fraser, Brann Garvey

1 2 3 4 5 6 12 11 10 09 08 07

Printed in the United States of America

TABLE OF CONTENTS

The Library of Doom is the world's largest collection of strange and dangerous books. The Librarian's duty is to keep the books from falling into the hands of those who would use them for evil purposes.

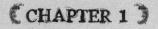

CHAPTER 1

THE DARK LIBRARY

The **Library of Doom** is dark.

The stairways are silent.

Cobwebs hang across the doors.

The Library's gardens are filled with weeds and `creeping` vines.

Floors are covered with broken glass.

Somewhere, boots `crunch` on the broken glass.

A shadow walks through the hallways.

It is the **Librarian**.

CHAPTER 2

THE LIBRARIAN

He is cold and tired, but he is glad to be home.

The Librarian looks down at his hands.

The Librarian has come back
with a handful of new books.

The Librarian has been gone for
a long time.

He has traveled over mountains and crossed deserts of ice.

He has fought many battles with strange creatures.

He has **discovered** books that no one else has seen for hundreds of years.

The books are filled with terrible **powers.**

Now, the Librarian is home.

The Librarian smiles. He is looking
forward to being in his own place.

He is looking forward to having a long rest.

He passes through a **huge** door and walks up the stairs toward his room.

The moonlight makes strange **shadows on the stairs.**

When he reaches the top step, the Librarian frowns. He makes a fist.

The door to his room
has been ripped away.

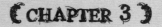

❰ CHAPTER 3 ❱

THE MISSING BOOKS

The Librarian runs through
the hole in the door.

He enters his room.

A wind blows
across the pages of
his books and papers.
The window has been
smashed.

A  has
been here.

The Librarian runs
to a special shelf where
he keeps his most
dangerous books.

The lock is smashed.
The books are missing.

19

The Librarian knows that one of his **powerful enemies** has taken the books.

Scattered pages lead up a stairway. They are pages from the missing books.

"I must find the books," the Librarian tells himself, "or the world is in **terrible danger**."

The pages pass out of a window and curve down into the **deep darkness**.

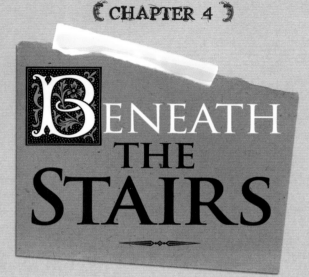

CHAPTER 4

BENEATH THE STAIRS

The Librarian stands on the sill of his window.

He puts his hands at his side, takes a deep breath, and jumps.

He falls through the air like a **heavy book**.

The Librarian falls through rooms that he has forgotten.

Staircases and balconies flash past him. Statues stare at him.

After many minutes, the Librarian lands at the very bottom of the library.

His boots scrape against old stones.

He follows the trail of pages through **twisting halls**.

When he turns a corner, the Librarian sees a great hole in the wall. The trail of pages disappears into the hole.

In front of the hole crouches a beast made of books.

CHAPTER 5

THE BEAST OF BOOKS

The beast is half man and half book and half octopus. The creature made of three halves roars.

Its long tongue rolls out. Its long arms unfold like hundreds of pages.

The Librarian jumps back.

Then the creature shoots out `jets of ink`. A cloud of darkness fills the room and blinds the Librarian.

From behind him, long arms grab his waist.

The Librarian is **squeezed** by the creature's powerful arms.

Quickly, the Librarian holds up his hands.

A **powerful light** flashes from his fingers. A blast of heat rips through the `inky cloud`.

The beast crumples into torn pieces of paper.

The Librarian closes his eyes.
He takes a deep breath and then
stands up.

He must find the missing books.

He steps into the dark hole.

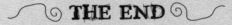 **THE END**

A PAGE FROM
THE LIBRARY
OF DOOM

LIBRARIES

The Library of Congress in Washington, DC, United States, contains more than 25 million books. It also has 4 million maps and 12 million photographs on file.

The world's most overdue library book was borrowed from a British university in 1668. The book was returned in 1956 but no fine was charged!

The Library of Alexandria in Egypt was considered the greatest library of ancient times. It held more than 700,000 rolls of paper, which is how books were written then.

In 1731, Benjamin Frankin opened the world's first "members only" library. Thanks to Ben, people still use library cards.

DAHL, MICHAEL.

BEAST BENEATH THE STAIRS

DATE DUE	BORROWER'S NAME	250001 ROOM NUMBER
1/12	Eddie Poe	
1/26	Neil Gaiman	256
2/12	Lemony Snicket	111
2/26	J. K. ROWLING	102
3/14	H.P. Lovecraft	12A
3/23	Stephen King	315
4/13	Bob L. Stine	23
4/27	HARRY HOUDINI	200
5/12	Dav...	
5/25		

DAHL, MICHAEL.

BEAST BENEATH THE STAIRS

250001

LIBRARY OF DOOM

ABOUT THE AUTHOR

Michael Dahl is the author of more than 100 books for children and young adults. He has twice won the AEP Distinguished Achievement Award for his nonfiction. His Finnegan Zwake mystery series was chosen by the Agatha Awards to be among the five best mystery books for children in 2002 and 2003. He collects books on poison and graveyards, and lives in a haunted house in Minneapolis, Minnesota.

ABOUT THE ILLUSTRATOR

Patricia Moffett loves fantasy and horror. In fact, the building where she works in London was built by the man who designed the scary house in the classic 1963 ghost film, *The Haunting*. Moffett used the building as the inspiration for her illustrations of the Library of Doom. She enjoys designing book covers and reading mythology and science fiction.

GLOSSARY

balconies (BAL-kuh-neez)—platforms on the outside of a building. Balconies are usually high above the ground and have railings.

clinging (KLING-ing)—holding on tightly

creeping (KREEP-ing)—growing and spreading over a surface, like a vine

crumple (KRUM-pul)—to shrink and break down, like an empty balloon

twisted (TWIS-tid)—curved and turning, bent out of shape

DISCUSSION QUESTIONS

1. The Librarian keeps the most dangerous books in the world locked up in his library. What do you think makes these books so dangerous? Can a book really be dangerous? Explain.

2. The Library of Doom is the largest library in the world. It is also the strangest. Would you want to visit it? Why or why not? Would you go alone, or would you want someone to go with you?

3. At the end of the story, the Librarian steps through the hole in the wall. Where is he going? What do you think happens next?

WRITING PROMPTS

1. The Librarian has returned to the Library of Doom after many adventures and battles. The author gives a few clues about what might have happened during those travels. Write your own story describing one of the Librarian's unknown adventures.

2. The beast beneath the stairs is made of books. Draw a picture of a creature made from objects you might find in a classroom. Then write a description of the creature. What does it eat? How does it sleep? Is it dangerous or tame? Does it make noises? How does it smell?

INTERNET SITES

Do you want to know more about subjects related to this book? Or are you interested in learning about other topics? Then check out FactHound, a fun, easy way to find Internet sites.

Our investigative staff has already sniffed out great sites for you!

Here's how to use FactHound:

1. Visit *www.facthound.com*

2. Select your grade level.

3. To learn more about subjects related to this book, type in the book's ISBN number: **1598893238**.

4. Click the **Fetch It** button.

FactHound will fetch the best Internet sites for you!